The Ghettobirds

The Ghettobirds

Bryant O'Hara

Frayed Edge Press
Philadelphia, PA

Published by Frayed Edge Press in 2021

Frayed Edge Press
PO Box 13465
Philadelphia, PA 19101

http://frayededgepress.com

Cover illustration by wassaykhan
Cover concept by Mark Conner

Publisher's Cataloging-in-Publication Data

Names: O'Hara, Bryant.
Title: The ghettobirds / Bryant O'Hara.
Description: Philadelphia, PA : Frayed Edge Press, 2021.
Identifiers: LCCN 2021932548 | ISBN 9781642510355 (pbk.) | ISBN
    9781642510362 (ebook)
Subjects: LCSH: Afrofuturism. | American poetry – 21st century. | Ameri-
    can poetry -- African American authors. | Science fiction poetry, Ameri-
    can. | BISAC: POETRY / American / African American | FICTION /
    Science Fiction / Alien Contact.
Classification: LCC PS309.F35 O33 2021| DDC 811 --dc22
LC record available at https://lccn.loc.gov/2021932548

Contents

Acknowledgements

So many people and organizations played important roles in the creation of this collection. Here are the ones to whom I am especially grateful:

To Professor Louis Curran and the WPI Men's Glee Club—for teaching me the power of the human voice.

To Stone Montgomery and the Thurman-Hamer-Ellington Percussion Choir—for resurrecting the rhythm I never thought I had.

To the members of the Klub Kuumba Collective—for providing the literary soil from which my voice could spring.

To the members of the Eyedrum Writers Exchange and the Decatur Sci-Fi/Fantasy/Horror Scribes—for honing that voice.

To Edward Austin Hall and Lee Furey—for their excellent work editing and proofreading this collection.

To Kevin Sipp and Mark Conner—for their artistic and musical contributions.

To my wife Alice—for constantly reminding me I was a poet as well as a husband and father.

To my brother Gregory—who told me what a ghettobird was.

Bad Mother

Nature is a bad mother—
half-raising one bastard species after another,
dropping them into an ongoing explosion,
saying, "Pfft, make your way,"
after sashaying down the eons
to drop off a load of kids.

These children of the deoxyribonucleic
constantly get themselves into a whole mosaic
of devilment, more often because
they were in the right place
that became the wrong place
at Nature's hard-luck dice roll.

And there's always a group of these hellions—
sometimes just one—
that manages to really foul the nest.
From the first anaerobic bacterium that messed
up the atmosphere, farting out oxygen,
to that whippersnapper Humankind—
some of them *really* get themselves in a bind.

And you know what Mama Nature always says?
"You fix it or you buy it—
I ain't got time for yo' bullshit,"
after sashaying down the eons
to drop off a load of kids.

A lot of them do buy it,
or jerry-build an adaptation,
but Humankind—oh, no …
This little knucklehead actually has the indignation

to talk back to its Mama like it's *grown*,
to get up in her face
and raise its voice at her,
saying,

"I'll fix it—
and I'll break this world to do it
if I have to.
And then I'm getting off this rock—
I've got better places to be
than under a couple o' meters of deep blue sea
'cause *I* ain't got time for *your* bullshit!"

And Nature, bad mutha that she is,
looks Humankind in its collective eyes,
and says,
"I dare you."

Mariah Pariah

Ladies and gentlemen—brothers and sisters—introducing …
MARIAH PARIAH!
Psychokinetic canary Carrie,
human screech owl on crack!
Tweeting to that shakalakaBOOMBOOMBOOM
’til yo’ body blows,
and yo’ soul slows
like spirit sap.

LIVE!
FROM THE GHOST OF THE GEORGIA DOME!
IT’S AMERICA’S
FAVORITE
50 FOOT WILE BLACK CHILE!

Can you feel her?
Can you feel her hips
swaying like a great-great grandma clock
with a
Tiki-tiki boom-boom,
Tiki-tiki boom-boom-boom,
Tiki-tiki boom-boom,
Tiki-tiki boom-boom-boom

Brothers and sisters, she is only an image—
writhing with a honey sweet life
that is not her life
but *your* life.
So go ahead—watch her—that is what you want.
Watch her destroy your city in one moonlit night.
Can you feel her?
Can you feel her hips

swaying like a great-great grandma clock
with a
Tiki-tiki boom-boom,
Tiki-tiki boom-boom-boom,
Tiki-tiki boom-boom,
Tiki-tiki boom-boom-boom

Listen to her, listen …
Hear her voice rising,
the decibels racing,
the capacitors charging in her throat,
and the song that's
taking you higher
and higher
and higher
and

Can you feel her?
Can you feel her hips
swaying like a great-great grandma clock
with a
Tiki-tiki boom-boom,
Tiki-tiki boom-boom-boom,
Tiki-tiki boom-boom,
Tiki-tiki boom-boom-boom

Can you feel her?
… as the windows fall …
Can you feel her hips
… as the doors fall …
swaying like a great-great grandma clock
… as the walls fall …
with a Tiki-tiki boom-boom …
… as the city …

… falls …
with a Tiki-tiki boom-boom-boom

Now … all that apocalypse can be yours!
For the price of a dollar a day,
you too can scrape your nerves
to the orgasmic warbles of Mariah Pariah.
And yes, we have the wearable version
for all you closet fans.

Can you feel her?
Can you feel her hips
swaying like a great-great grandma clock
with a
Tiki-tiki boom-boom,
Tiki-tiki boom-boom-boom,
Tiki-tiki boom-boom,
Tiki-tiki boom-boom-boom

20,000 terabytes of heart-thrashing soul
from a $2,000 box
and a two-bit concept
just two feet from your eyes!
Yours, for the trivial price
of a piece of your soul
for general consumption.

Sym-Bionic

We have the technology.
We can rebuild you.
We can make you a watch
or a watchmaker,
a satellite
or a technician.
We can rebuild you
from the ground down
or the ground up.
Which way do you want to go?
Simple
or complex?

It will take time,
but since we have the technology,
we have the time.

We can rebuild a poet barely alive
into a socially acceptable unit
with a V-6 engine
and turbocharged overhead cams!

Hang on, poetry fans,
we're going for a ride …

Picture this—
no,
better yet,
let us picture it for you:
Your mouth is open,
metal showing
the machine within.

You are begging for a kiss—
someone to kiss the machine—
it will improve your smile.
We have the technology to smile.
We are the intimate
and the intricate.

We can rebuild you.
We can take you apart.

This won't hurt a bit.
Smile.
This won't hurt a bit.
This is the rage.
Can you picture your smile?
Your mouth open,
you have something to say,
of course,
but we have to be
really
close
to you
to hear it …
as close as your organs.
We have to coil
into you
to hear
that message.

You'll notice
we need
no batteries now.
It's a symbiotic thing;
you won't understand

till we're already
hitched.

Don't worry,
this won't hurt a bit;
just sit back and
relax.
This is the good thing
about the technology we are.
We can see
the machine
within us.

It is time you saw yours.

The Music Is Always On

The frostbite dies away once the bass drops. These old ARP 2600s run pretty smooth when the temperature's below 50. This is the day the big data dump from the Europa probes goes online. My hands warm as I caress dials and twist static out of a patch cable. The ARP provides the seed rhythm; my algorithms water that seed with data and grow beats, lyrics, and composi- tions. Fragments of music blossom into hits like bosons shot out of a superconducting supercollider; they are as short-lived as they are hot.

And there is more to come,
for the music is always on.

Ever since Jo Effington mashed up the Arecibo Observatory's decades-long data stream into the world's longest drum-n-bass composition, every musical hacker with a freak on for radio as- tronomy, getting teary while watching *Cosmos*, has been clogging up the Internet with songs that literally take a lifetime to listen to.

And here's the tricked-out, somehow not quite played-out, old- hat thing: these songs *evolve*. The ones that hit the top of the charts—most of those actually take days to sink into you. That is the new music—that is the music of lives that are now very, very long. Somewhere in this world there is a musician/hacker who will take all your social data and turn it into a soundtrack. And it will never end. And the biofeedback-based symphonies are making a comeback after a brief flash in the late 2050s.

Our lives are so noisy, so funky—so downright god-damned dance-able, you can take the electric slide straight into the grave. The goth set even came up with software that monitors your

rate of decay and mixes the chemical data with AI-sampled
video clips. Illegal as hell, but still, your corpse can not only
look beautiful but also sound beautiful.

My friend the guitarist hung up his ax after 30 years of touring.
Not because he was old (god, who cares about that nowadays).
Just wanted some peace and quiet, he said. So he went to a
mountaintop to turn down the volume.

It is a bit loud down here,
and the music is always on.

We call them The Birds, the young ones. They have a new
language that sounds like a vocoded modem missing the bands
needed to sound like human speech. Data passes between them
in packets picked up on their personal networks. Most of it is
encrypted, as far as we old folks are concerned—nothing but
noise leaks out. Fragments of data get translated as something
like birdcalls. Hence the name.

In colors that slide off the human spectrum, The Birds gather
in subway tunnels. One among them, staggering like a zombie,
opens her mouth. Squawks and electric screeches transform
into something that, still not speech, is but a torrent of words
as if from an aphasic gangsta rapper catching the holy ghost in
the middle of evening prayers. The Birds don't exactly follow
her but merely begin their own drunken counterpoint.

It cycles in the tunnels,
between us,
in the tunnels.
The music is always on.

Trapped in the logos, these kids occasionally sync up with each
other, and for a moment they are angels in a hoodoo choir,
where the rhythm rides them until a security drone tranqs the
MC. As fast-acting medication kicks in, the voices lap back
from the tidal pull. Without the drones, the flock would infect
those patrons with poor barriers—and the beat would go on.

Our internal Wi-Fi can still hear the seed rhythm that kicked
off the outbreak of song. You have to be disconnected—no,
you have to be dead nowadays for it to really be quiet.

We, the very old, wonder what The Birds do when the power
goes out.
They say little then, though we know they are not mute.
Perhaps they do it just to piss off the old folks.

Perhaps, underneath all that noise,
they are whispering to each other.
It is hard to tell.
The music is always on.

Riddim Revelations

Vulture, the Virus Riddim,
was a farmer of Big Data—
a musicological algorithm,
quite tenacious,
parsing through chord structures and bass loops,
through Jungle and Jingle,
Classical, Metal,
Polka, Bulgarian,
Mangue Bit and Bop.

At a critical mass
(what seemed to some a moment of insanity),
the Virus Riddim gazed
into the Musical Genome for days,
sucking down CPU cycles.
To humanity it declared itself … a critic,
that it had the computational sickles
to fix the vulnerabilities.

I will not hesitate, it said,
to hone humanity's flow.

Despite the exhortations of the purists,
this dispassionate de-composer
laid bare the math and the metadata—
the souls of the Musical Genome.

And so began the sensuous disintegration
of melody and syncopation.
This Vulture, this Virus Riddim,
chewed through our remedial music
like a tiller through the soil,

planting seed rhythms
whose algorithms
had script kiddies stumped
and true hackers cackling.

Sure, scratch the records, said the hackers.
Send us mixtapes when you're done.

Play on, child of Humankind.
Play on.

Heavy Cranes

Who am I?
A casual human.
I dabble in humanity.
Call me Joseph No-One—
my enemies call me Nobody,
my friends call me Nobody Special.

On the third day of Kwanzaa
a mass of circuit diagrams
zigzagged up to me,
and slouching in the next chair
made me an offer
to be more
than I alone
could ever become.

He said, "You—yes, you, a dabbler in humanity—
can be a part of the army of its saviors.
We are the Ghettobirds,
singularities born in slums.
We deep-dream of stars,
and we offer you our services as Heavy Cranes."

"Heavy Cranes, huh?"

"Sure … you see,
building worlds is easy.
It's the people that are hard to work with.
You gotta go for the minds.
You can't just tell 'em
to follow the drinking gourd;
you gotta get 'em to get up off the planet,

and head straight for the Big Dipper.
 "And remember—
we must take our worlds with us.

'Cause sometimes
it's gotta be small enough
to fit inside your helmet,
and grand enough
to build a starship."

"So … I'm gonna be a pilot of one these Heavy Cranes?"

"No … think of yourself
more along the lines
of a universal joint
than a pilot."

"Wait—what? Why're you doin' this?
"What's in it for you?"

"Look into my circuitry
and you will see human souls
driving it like they stole it.

My motivation is simple:
it is the many of you that make me."

"Interesting offer. Got a guarantee?"

"As always … no."

"Least you're honest.
You got yourself a U-joint.
How do we start?"

"Just hold our hands."

So I held the Heavy Crane's hands,
and four more gathered around me.
Their circuitry wrapped around my nerves
as their struts and gears and geegaws
linked themselves to my body
and to each other's,
and before you could say, "Transform!"
I had become
a Ghettobird,
a Heavy Crane.

Our first task
was to resurrect the junky-jellymen.
In this city of
run-down dreams,
crook-lights,
and evil-dead hoopties,
dirty syringes sang:

Let's go out to the crackhouse,
Let's go out to the crackhouse,
Let's go out to the crackhouse,
And grab ourselves some smack!

And the junky-jellymen and women
wiggled and jiggled
to the jingle
as the jabberwocks
on their backs
fed the volts
to their backbrains.

I and the other Heavy Cranes
took metal,
old computer parts,
and invoked the power of
Shaft,
Shaka,
and Fred G. Sanford
to build skeletons
for these unstructured ones.

My first case
was one Minnie the Moocher.
Most slapped-together,
ghetto-rigged job
I've ever done …
but the bones did power up.
They slipped under her skin
and began converting the jabberwock
into a backup power source.

As Minnie the Moocher awoke from her slumber.
I packed away my geegaws,
assumed human form, and made her the offer.

Like a professional dabbler in humanity,
she asked for a guarantee.

Like a newborn Heavy Crane, I said flatly,
"There ain't one."

She dug my architecture
and asked for the howto.

We held hands ,,,

"Remember this—
We got a small world in our hands—
so keep it under your helmet."

"Who do we give it to?"

"Everyone."

In the Era of the Silent

A pair of Ghettobirds came for Ol' Preacher Bag Lady at Five Points Station, Eastbound to Indian Creek.

One of them, a mechanical chimera with a tall, feminine figure, a hawk's head, wasp wings, and a kaleidoscopic breastplate, hovered over Ol' Preacher Bag Lady. Its head was not composed of feathers but of something like patch cables matted in layers down her head and back.

The other, a male of similar design, with an owl's head, came up to me, prompting the loyal patrons of mass transit to mass exit stage anyplace-else-but-where-I-was-standing, which was rooted to the station floor.

The male's head turned—just like an owl's—as it examined me with eyes the color of channel static. When its head righted, a seam formed down the middle, and the head split, revealing a black man in sepia tones, his face obscured by an origami mask made of what looked like interlocking pieces of metal.

"I am Ras Elegba, the Ghettobird of crossroads," said the face within the face within the face. "And we have a question to ask."

Ol' Preacher Bag Lady was damning Ras Elegba's companion like the battle-axe I'd grown to know and … well, not love, but at least tolerate. The female Ghettobird was at least two heads taller than her, but that didn't stop Ol' Preacher Bag Lady.

"You better get behind me, Satan! I ain't 'fraid of you! I'm right with God, and he's right here with me …."

She kept that up until the Ghettobird shot her with a dart. Downed her like a dog, I thought. I never liked the crazy biddy, but damn ….

"Your question, great sir, is this: Is this woman a dog, or is she a fox? Your lives are tied here at this station, on this line, and now, at this time. Answer honestly."

"What'll happen to the old woman?"

"My mate is Yolanda Light-and-Water, the Ghettobird of dreams. And she is asking the elder a question."

The female Ghettobird was extruding silk threads from her jaws, covering Ol' Preacher Bag Lady from her head to her waist. Thin rods protruded from the Ghettobird's cheeks to knit a shroud over Ol' Preacher Bag Lady's head. That was too intimate a conversation, so I turned away.

The male Ghettobird and I took a seat on a bench. The station announced the Eastbound line was temporarily suspended.

"Dogs and foxes are family, just different branches," I said. "The only difference that matters to people is that dogs are useful. Foxes don't guard henhouses. Dogs do."

"Humans have shaped dogs into hundreds of breeds," said Ras Elegba. "Some are work dogs. Some are mere toys. Many more are accidental combinations—mutts. Are all dogs useful?"

"By themselves, no. But in general, dogs and humans have been together for thousands of yrears. We're like a married couple that's known each other since we were toddlers."

"Then what of the fox?"

"Foxes have their place in the world. They may not always be welcome, but they keep their part of the ecosystem in balance. And their behavior has become a description of how humans can sometimes behave. To call someone "a fox" or "foxy" is often a compliment or an expression of admiration."

"So, are foxes useful?"

"To a degree; depends on the context. But then, that applies to dogs, too."

Ol' Preacher Bag Lady was covered from her head to her chest in Yolanda Light-and-Water's thick, silk shroud.

I stood and faced Ras Elegba. "She's a fox. To me. Based on what I know of her. I'd known her for years, and she irritated the hell out of me. But damned if she isn't persistent. She, among others, made me glad to be an atheist. A 'conversion unit,' I called her. Someone who tries to talk her way into people's heads, trick them into subscribing to God."

"She is a virus then? Should my mate kill her?"

"What? No!"

"But she is of no use to you. In fact, she's a threat."

"She's a pain in the ass, and I don't like her, but that doesn't mean other people don't." Yolanda had stopped weaving the shroud and looked at me with the same channel-static eyes as her mate. She retracted the knitting rods and wiped her mouth.

"Who knows, maybe by shaking people up, pissing them off,

she actually helps them. Makes them aware of themselves.
People do talk when Ol' Preacher Bag Lady's around."
"You have said enough. We can finish your recycling now."
From the corner of my left eye, I saw another body being
shrouded.

Mine.

By Ras Elegba.

My colon clenched. I turned to what I thought was Ras Elegba,
and asked, "Am I dreaming?"

"No. Just distracted. Just like the old woman."

"So you came for both of us?"

"Yes," said Ras Elegba. His outer face reassembled itself into
the scrap-metal owl head. "Do you want to know what Yolanda
asked the old woman?"

"Yes. Please."

"The same question."

"And what was her answer?"

"The same."

Something like a warm ball expanded in my stomach, waiting
for release.

I let the Ghettobird change me, and the warmth seemed to
burst from my navel as if out of a firehose, leaving me empty.

I slept and waited for the metamorphosis.

I slept and waited for the coming of my name.

Anticipation, Intimate and Intricate

I remember your hair around that pole
on the night after the naming
of the newest Ghettobird.

I could see you blazing in the infrared
as I packed away my souls.
That is what I call them,
the nodules and gewgaws
that sprout from my back and head
like some symbiotic fungi.

We had a lovely conversation.
And I will always remember the wind
wrapping your hair,
embracing the light post,
an exercise in intimacy
and fluid dynamics.

I know what you desire,
and as much as I ache
to show you the world of the recombined,
I wait.

The waiting period exists for a reason.
It takes great strength to die.
It takes great strength to die and grow again.

The Dreams from Mistren Peachtree Street

Every Third Thursday,
the sentient
street-corner
camera networks
condense themselves
into an Ultraviolet Market,
well past black—
a bazaar built of bizarre mathematics—
trafficking data
sporked from human souls.

These more-than-Streets pimp-walk
among the human talent,
deck themselves out
in differential equations
written in rhinestone.

Mistren Peachtree Street has hoq preferred traders:
Mister Buckhead barters his witching hour brawl footage,
Madam Little Five Points her happy hour loli-goths,
Mistren West End hoq smiling hour hip-hop warriors.

Ah, but on this night,
I, Woxy Wub-Wub, Ghettobird of Hustles,
have an urge to splurge—
I, too, shall go to the market.

Third Thursday,
and I toss a two-finger salute
to a blindered blue plexiglass eye
of Mistren Peachtree Street
at a fork in hoq asphalt that

splits into the human hive
and the almighty superhighways.

I give hoq my best knowing smile—
a little something for the market—
blow a kiss with wintry fresh breath,
and ease on
down hoq sidewalk
in the butt-end
of a polar vortex—
So sayeth the smartassphone.

Every high-hat tap-tap of a hostess's heels,
Every rumble of balding racing tires,
Every hurly-burly trundle of heavy transit
is a multidimensional snapshot—a sensory gem—
worth something very high
in a currency very strange
to buyers very much unknown—
at least to the televised talent.

The more-than-Streets hawk their wares in the open,
calling out product specs
in the cadence of hymns.
The market thrives,
the talent is blind to it
(wrong spectrum—so sad)
(so many things are …).

We Ghettobirds, as always, keep mum.
This is the market of the camera-hives—
Our money's no good here,
but the drinks are free.

What the more-than-Streets call "souls"
is not what the talent call "souls",
nor what we Ghettobirds call "souls."
There is no exchange rate yet—
nothing in common
defined to anyone's satisfaction.

So, we post-folks settle for packets of moments.
We haggle.
We shrug.
We trade.
I look forward to the haggle, the selling of sizzle,
the bullshit, the banal talent-dreams.

The more-than-Streets have their own dreams,
and someday we might know them ...
as well as we know our own.

The Solarium Garden

In the hard sunshine of the 22nd century,
three sisters,
the Mistress Engineers,
boogie down in a dance club
on a shepherd moon of Jupiter—
airlock to airlock downed
with ever-clean shag.

The music is data,
distilled from the planet's centuries-long storms.
It is damn funky,
and damn radioactive,
but it is all good:
The music, like the club, is unfiltered—
only the Adapted can get up on that dance floor.

They dance and
they dream,
sashay
until they beam
as they dance and
they dream.

Hips sway,
legs gleam,
backs bend
as these mistresses' many-placed minds
begin the dance to attend to their
asteroid garden,
balanced between gravity wells.

"Dream in the physical," they say as they play.

Dandelion, dressed in green and white,
break-dances while building paths for probes,
(She aims for the gathering places: the Trojan points, the Kui-
per Belt.)
Paprika, dressed in green and crimson,
does the Pony, slowly, in low gravity
and corrects trajectories.
(She calls out coordinates, and the dance floor hollers.)

Sorrel, dressed in green and ochre,
spins and prays to invented gods in Old Esperanto.
(She does the deep survey, seeking brown dwarfs.)

"This garden, oblivious,
will feed us,
and someday free us,"
the sisters say.

Dandelion pirouettes
while juggling plumbers' wrenches,
adjusting mass drivers,
steering ancient rock
to their garden of stone:
the Solarium Garden.

Paprika leads hexapod assemblers
in the electric slide,
smelting, separating,
weaving rock
into bigger machines
to build bigger machines.

Sorrel does the Hammer dance,
dreaming of boring into dirty ice,

pushing slush to the surface,
molding big spaces for little places.

"This garden, unconscious,
will be us,
and someday free us,"
the sisters say.
The Mistress Engineers clasp hands,
And the Adapted follow suit,
Forming a circle,

They shut their eyes and turn, turn, turn …

In waking dreams,
Paprika sculpts a hollowed-out asteroid into a city.

In lucid dreams,
Dandelion connects the sleeping stone to its senses.

In vivid dreams,
Sorrel fires up the factories,
blows a whistle that makes its way
around the solar system.

Pocketful of posies—
ashes, ashes,
we all
fall …

"This garden, luscious,
will flee us,
and someday free us,"
the sisters say.

And that will be a glorious day.

Hoop Dance

for Baba Askia Toure: Here are the stars …

Ras Elegba,
Speaker for the Recombined,
Mother-and-Father of Starships,
yawns
and greets the dawn.

He watches his fingers and arms
grow a little longer
and a little thinner
as he completes his slide
into feminine form
for the 50-year Boogie.

Every half century,
the Ghettobirds
start their grand dance cycle
at the Gaian Ring,
in geosynchronous Earth orbit,
known affectionately as
The Hoop.

They do this
for what they call
the recycling of souls—
and they never stop.

For them it is always Carnival.

Now complete,
she calls me

while I am under Ganymede,
asks me to paint her vèvè.

"Helluva time for a booty call, man," I reply.
The old joke takes its time to reach her—
and she is patient:
I resonate at this honor,
Been a while
since Ras was female,
so I hightail it in style
on a laser-launched cruise ship.

I catch her preparing for the long dance.
The electronic paint spreads
to make vèvè
that are ancient and modern,
visual and … other.

They form just a portion
of her part
of the Great Circuit.
Acolytes from across the Genus
come to trace their own
loving pathways upon her,
completing her.

With a kiss
she passes on to me
the keys to the instruction-set
and the tradition-set
of the Genus,
and I …
I go away for a while,
leaving behind
this derivative: your narrator.

I am a fiction in this dance—
all of us are.

The vèvè show that.
The vèvè see to that.

The dance opens
with old traveling songs,
ancient blues,
and datasets from probes.
They get woven into pirouettes,
low-gravity jetés,
and good old-fashioned rump-shakin'.

Ras is not all here when she sings.
None of us are.
The songs
and the data spooning them
shout that
and see to that.

There are different names
for the ceremony:
In the colonies,
we call it the BounceWiggle;
in The Hoop—
the Hula,
of course.

The songs
and the data
and the wonder
and the spirit
call the restless all
who feel they have no city.

Come with us,
say the songs,
and build the traveling city.

We seek the path to come,
say the datasets,
and go.
We seek
the one
to which
to go.
As the Ghettobirds dance,
we writhe
in the synaptic bath
of sense data.

It is—
to baselines—
a hurricane toggling the Divinity bit.

It is—
to the enhanced—
a wind driving us all to the leaving place.

It is—
to the recombined—
working up another sweat in a century's work.

It is all
sleight of hand
once you cozy up to the universe,
let her whisper open secrets
into whatever receives signal.

At the last degree of The Hoop,
the Ghettobirds raise their arms,
fingers always pointing
to the same point
on the galactic map.
They unpack titanium bats
and swing them
to the music of the dance,
as if aiming an imaginary ball
at that point.
They pound the ground
in percussive polyrhythms—
pulling
at a paradigm
like a dog
in heat
on a chain.

Every other measure
they slam the ends on the ground.

"So *be* it,"
say the bats.
"Pick a point in the sky
and we will go to it."

We build a starship
at the last degree
of The Hoop.
And we dance while we do it,
singing
as we weave its minds together
from uploaded patterns
of spectators
and dancers.

Its body begins
in the Lagrange points
of Earth and Luna,
and make their way
to The Hoop.

The dance moves to the ship,
a half-built megalopolis,
and it spirals out toward,
and then past,
the Lagrange point shepherd moons.

The ship Hohmann-transfers
out of the system,
stopping often along the way.
It's an All-Souls Train,
whistling in the radio spectrum,
"Now boarding!"

Launch is not the coda of the dance.
It is the repeat sign.

Call it what moves you:
the recycling of souls;
the cycle of the Genus.
It is the way we roll,
here in Long Now.

I wave goodbye
to my self that grows
into the next Speaker for the Recombined,
the next Mother-and-Father of Starships.

As we launch,
Ras Elegba speaks for our templates
and for our children left behind:

"We remember this little whorl of worlds—
and rejoice,
for we are all genus Human.
And in our cosmically,
comically
short time …
we are immortal."

"Remember,
and rejoice."

Cornelius, of the Rock

You hear the howl
before you hear the hum
before you hear the huff
before you hear the hush ...
That is the Cornelius,
the fantastic, phantasmic Bankhead Line,
sliding into the station
on a Gaussian groove.

The doors of the last three cars of the Bankhead Line are
never open. Those last three cars are always dark, always in use,
always inviting a quick sidewise glance. No one may enter them,
except from the inside.

No one you know knows who will go to the back. They always
pack a bag, the size of a kindergartener's. They clutch each bag
so tightly ... like a lost childhood toy.
They empty wallets of change if they are wealthy, cell phones if
they are chatty, spirits if they believe in such things. The discon-
nection is a ceremony each invents while making their way to
the back.

The fourth car from the last is loudest, full of revelers and
drunkards, street preachers and scientists.

As the Cornelius makes its way to its momentary terminus, a
chant rises from end to oh, so coveted end:

Cornelius, of The Rock [The Rock] —
Soultrain ...
stone carver ...
Cornelius, of The Rock [The Rock] —

Wandering
mind of the
tunnel-boring
WhirlyWyrm …
Cornelius, of The Rock [The Rock]
Maker of ways out of walls,
Take us to the line.
Take us to the line.
Take us the end of the end of the line …

They all want a glimpse of the momentary terminus,
And they will never get it:
the spores from the third dark car
sing to them,
and bring to them
a fuzzy, out-of-focus frenzy …
a buzz, and then ecstasy,
and from that daze,
there is a phase change,
and then the hymn:

Howl,
Hum,
Huff, and
Hush …
Cornelius,
see in us
the future, luscious. …

Howl,
Hum,
Huff, and
Hush …
Cornelius

sees in us
the dangerous,
the precious,
the Howl,
Hum,
Huff, and
Hush …

Cornelius,
free in us
the luscious …
future …

The door to the third dark car slides open.
There is blank moment.

The door shuts.

A pastel blue bike stands with tempera blue rims—missing its
rider,

A tablet, screen down—short a subscriber,

A rattle—minus a child.
The mother and father wail, and then howl.

And the Soultrain howls back,
long and loud.
As the howl decays into the hum,
pops into the huff,
falls into the hush,
a giggle,
hidden in the hush,
does a little rise
and does a little fall.

The doors open—last stop before the lost stop,
the momentary terminus.

All passengers must leave the Soultrain.

The remnants of the missing are left on board.
These things are not lost,
and the Cornelius wastes nothing …
and the owners may …
may …
Maybe in some other way …

But that is not for us to say.

The Silent Station

"We will have your attention."
"We will have your attention."

The voice was not the voice of the familiar,
grumpy dispatch lady,
deigning to tell us
a train is somewhere, somehow, broken—
this voice belonged
to a larynx that had other places to be.

"We will have your attention."
"We will have your attention."

"Vine City Station has gone silent."
"Vine City Station has gone silent -"
"gone to meet its namesake"
"in the newly networked earth."

That did not stop the train from arriving.
On any other line,
this would have been out of line,
but this is Bankhead, home of mad MARTA—
her ecosystem was—and is—
still young and full of surprises.

I enter,
like all commuters
heading anyplace besides the terminus,
with headphones on,
focused on nothing as much as possible.

Rule #1—Always wear headphones.

"We will have your attention."
"We will have your attention."

"Vine City Station has gone silent."
"Vine City Station has gone silent."

"Do not approach the doors."
"Do not attempt to exit the cars."
"Do not approach the doors.
"Do not leave the cars."

The train stopped, and the doors opened.
The platform, dusty
like nature held a concert
and all the plants were invited.
People stood, waiting,
all staring at something
none of us could see.

Many of them were moving ever so slowly.
The pollen settled on them.

Phones sounded off
like bees hitting wind chimes.

I picked up.

No one spoke.

"We will have your attention."
"We will have your attention."
The voice was in my headphones.

"You will move when we say you will move"

"Do not look out the window."
"Do *not* look out the window …"
it was taunting me, daring me to disobey it.

An accidental glance, and then I could not look away.
I saw something in the window
that reminded me of the alien
but not really alien
biology of slime molds:
complex, pulsating filaments and globules

Rule #2—Do not disobey the voice.

I could hear someone
sitting beside me in the dark.
The person was warm—
really warm,
and there was a slight odor of …
mold?
I couldn't tell.

Rule #3—Never look a passenger in the eye unless that person
speaks to you.

"Do I have your attention?"
"Do I have your attention?"

It was …
I don't know what it was.
It was a beautiful voice—
masculine, feminine, I'm still not sure.
It was not processed—
it was … controlled.

The voice slipped past my headphones,
was whispering in my ear.
I made a motion for my ears,
then looked down—
my headphones were in my lap.

"Not those doors."
"Go to the next car."

These notes I leave for the next passenger.

Forgive my chicken scratch—
I don't have much time.

I'm going someplace strange,
and I don't think I'll be back.

Pigeon Police

Don't mess with the pigeons that wear
the black double-breasted jackets—
The cops those birds call have claws.
These officers are beautiful,
but you cannot touch them.
They have a powerful defense,
and they are part of a machine ecosystem—
and that system does not give a damn
about your too-loud conversation.
The pigeons are polite, but firm.
The K-9-2s will taze, bag, and tag your ass.

The animals you see in the station nowadays,
most of them are unreal:
rats are the maintenance crew,
monitoring and repairing the cars and the rails,
resurrecting the jumpers that hit the third rail.
Mechanical roaches keep the real ones in line.

The Pigeon Police are who most of us talk to,
and they are friendly enough.
They will get close to you,
start up conversations.
Children love them and feed them.
The Pigeon Police regurgitate the scraps
for their flesh-and-blood templates.

The rules of the station are simple,
posted everywhere,
and are not suggestions.
The system has its ways of maintaining order,
some subtle, some blunt.

As long as you do not break the law,
you will reach your destination.
As long as the ecosystem does not evolve past the laws,
we can all be content.

               Bryant O'Hara

The Dyson Tree's Promise

In the melancholy gravity
of a scorched gas giant,
doing a cold, tight tango
'round a burned-out star,
a tree
rooted in an icy moon,
bred for hard vacuum,
basking in gamma rays,
sings a long ditty
to itself
as it dances,
as it dreams …

An automated search heard its whistling,
redundant and dense,
full of melody and data.

Our poet,
a Cloud-dwelling number-cruncher,
took a decade to decode it,
understand it,
then feel it,
be at peace with it,
and express it.

This
is the header
from the mecha-poet:

[[BEGIN]]

[I have never put my hope in any other … any other …]

#%
I'm not tired, though I should be.
My arms don't fold the way they used to.
My hands have become filaments
to catch lightning from a gas giant,
and I am an artery,
a tree,
fractal.
%#

[
I have never put my hope in any other …
any other but my mother star …
]

#%
I stand … albeit as a polyp
filled with conscious sand …
Eyes straight … on stalks
… to catch a wider spectrographic band …
Arms raised … in three hundred sixty directions,
… three dolorous dimensions …
Feet knotted into a history of a condensed, dead race
… into the intimate,
… the intricate,
… the life and the death and the breath and
%#

[
I have never put my hope in any other …
any other but my mother star …
]

#%
and yet I hold out my arms.
I hold out hope:
five trillion souls—
a grove
for a planet made
of ghosts.

I hold out our hope …
I hold out my hope …
%#

[I want to sleep,]

#% but I am always on. %#

[I want to close my eyes,]

#%
but I am awake and
I can never blink again.
%#

[
I want to blow out the fire
tickling my fingers,
]

#%
but five trillion voices
are laughing too loud.
%#

[I want to breathe,]

#%
but I am a closed system
falling around a gas giant
falling around a white dwarf.
%#

[I want to run,]

#%
but my roots run too deep
inside an underground ocean
of a modest-sized moon.
%#

[I want to walk away,]

#%
but trees in space don't walk.

So I hold out my hope,
waiting
and whistling
and wailing:
%#

#% [COME!] %#

#%
Use me for firewood!
See, and be warm.
Find me and warm me!
%#

[SPEAK!]

#% Dance, %#

[DRUM …]

#% Play, %#

[Stay …]

#%
Fly away,
and then be still.
%#

[… and then be still.]

#% [
I hold out hope,
howling into the void
so no soul will lose its way
because I did not hold out my burning hands
in this night.

In the wasteland, where one tree stands,
there is always—always—
the dream (at least the dream)
of a forest.
] %#

#%
I have never put my hope in any other …
any other but my mother star …
I hold out trillions of hopes,
pass them on,
and scatter them.
%#

[In the name,]

#% In the spirit, %#

#% [
In the terra firma
of those dreams

I hold out my hope …
PASS … THEM … ON!
] %#

[
I hold out my thousand-eighty hands for all to see.
I hold my arms,
and I hold out.
I hold.
]

#% [
I have never put my hope in any other …
and I hold out hope …
I hold out hope …
I hold …
I hold …
I hold …
] %#

[[END]]

In the bright, groovy gravity
of a ringed gas giant,
doing a long, exact slingshot
'round a bright yellow star,

a tree
rooted in an icy moon,
bred for hard vacuum,
basking in gamma rays,
sings a loving ditty
to a lonely little forest
as it dances,
as it dreams …

Soul, Encrypted

You are in there, somewhere,
somehow encrypted, hiding
melody in marrow,
sensuality in synapses,
hormones in howls.

You are in there, somewhere,
You are unique, unbreakable,
a cipher,
one of billions of ciphers out there,
and somewhere in there,
you are the one
holding something I need—
a gift,
a message
packed inside a smile.

You are in there, but where?
Am I laboring
under some sweet delusion?
Perhaps, in my passion,
I'll detect you,
like an event horizon
past which I cannot go,
or down a hole of illusions,
or a row too long to hoe.

I've both your keys but can't get in there.
"That's only fair," you say.
"To see, you let yourself be seen."

So take my keys—it's only fair.
Take a peek at me if you dare.
Open me up
and look for me,
in here,
somewhere,
I hope you find me—
in here or
in there.
I hope you find me,
somewhere,
someday.

The [OOV] Machine

We took the GRUMBLE out of the [G]roove,
We took the RECTILINEAR out of the [G][R]oove,
We took the ELECTROLYTIC out of the [G][R]oov[E] …
and we put it in a box …

We call it the [OOV] machine.

We took the GULLIBLE out of the [G]roove,
We took the RHEUMATOID out the [G][R]oove,
We took the EMPHYSEMIC out of the [G][R]oov[E] …
and we put it
in an
itty
bitty
box …

We call it the [OOV] machine.

So how do you start?

You palpate the box
until you hear a "pop."
That be the dongle …
You fondle the dongle
'til the nerves, knobs,
and nibbly-bits display.

Wait three seconds to play:

You can flick the switches with a slick finger,
Nibble the knobs until they nictitate,
Adjust the slider inside her …

Yeah, folks, *my* [OOV] machine is a "she" …

Now wait a minute …
Before you gender designators
get your pirated panties
into polka-dot knots,
remember
the [OOV] machine
is infinitely malleable:

You can
bend its
gender to render
any specification
on the spectrum of
DEEP
HUMAN
SATISFACTION.

We took the GRAVITAS out of the [G]roove,
We took the RAW out of the [G][R]oove,
We took the EMETIC out of the [G][R]oov[E] …
and we shoehorned that little fucker
into an enclosure
you can fit
in the palm
of your hand …
or wear as a piece of jewelry …
or snuggle …
deep into your colon …
as you smuggle it into prison.

It is the [OOV] machine …
You can take it anywhere—
it fits.

Now please note that
DEEP
HUMAN
SATISFACTION
is not guaranteed
[that is all you].
That cannot be guaranteed
for the [OOV] machine has no power.

It has no batteries—
it's all switches and dials
and the special sauce
that makes the [OOV] machine
make you go "Oooov …"

It is powered by,
well,
whatever name you
want to apply:
The funk,
mojo,
soul,
galvanic skin resistance,
the electrochemical bath
that your brain is swimming in …
the tiny thunderstorms
raging inside your body,
as predictable
as the weather outside you,
and just as
potent.

Children of the Woods

I watched my great, great grandchildren
sink into the earth—
and I cried,
and I cried,
and I cried.

I watched my great, great grandchildren
smiling and leaning to the left
as they descended into the bio/techno/mycosphere—
the grey and the green and the gooey
of the newly networked earth—
and I cried,
and I cried,
and I cried.

"I cannot go with you—
I don't have the filaments.
I cannot understand."

They sent me a text message,
ancient and quaint,
saying,
—Don't cry Poppy—
—We are alive (oh, so alive)—
—growing and wading deep, deep down—
—into Fungitown.—

—There is work to do here—
—deep, deep down in Fungitown—
—and we would take you, too—
—deep, deep down into Fungitown—
—but you cannot go.—

—You know this, right, Poppy?—
—It is not meant to be.—

—I know this—I text back
(my thumbs ache, my joints crack …
I don't have the filaments).

I can only see the wake of their movements,
translated by software two generations younger than me
that (I barely understand | I cannot understand).
Perhaps someday I may,
when my flesh decays
or my metal winds down.

—Won't you take me?—I ask.

—Down to Fungitown?—
—Sorry, Poppy, you're not "fungi" enough—

What's left of them coughs up spores as they laugh.
I chuckle as I cough.

—Put your mask on, Poppy—

I speak to their sinking bodies: "What are you doing down
there?
What are you building?
Are you eating?
Are you being eaten?
What *are* you?"

More spores, and then the texts:
—You wouldn't believe us if we told you.—
—Put your mask on, Poppy.—

—You can't take much more of this.—
—Watch your texts, Poppy. We'll see you. We will.—
—Not soon, but you will see us.—
—You will.—
—Until then, Poppy … live longer.—
—You will see us. Live longer.—
I watered my great, great grandchildren
when they sank into the earth—
and I cried,
and I cried,
and I cried—
not because they had died,
but out of pride.

Some day,
some thing—
some amazing, familiar,
and (oh, please) beautiful thing
will grow there.

I know this.
I know this.
I know this.

The Ocotillo Invasion

Utah cringes as hacked Ocotillo turn carnivorous,
spitting psychoactive pollen into the atmosphere,
dusting entire subdivisions.

The victims wander,
searching eagerly for where sunlight is strongest.
A part of their backbrain
gets tickled by the sun
at an angle their pituitary glands
have relearned to sense.

There have been reports that
the vision of pollen victims
has moved into the ultraviolet—
they wear sunglasses at raves
due to their newfound sensitivity.

In the afternoon, they wear welder's goggles.

It is Utah,
and it is so very bright there.

The Ocotillo and the pollen victims have built walking machines
with assistance from biohackers and wild, traitorous smiths
from all over the planet.
The machines look like the ghostly outlines of trees,
the roots modded into multitoed hooves.
Traces of rare earth magnets
have been detected inside the machines—
neodymium iron boron chief among them.

The root-hooves move with slow, deliberate rhythm,
as if the forest of four-bar linkages
were straining against the earth's flux.
The wind moves them.
The earth keeps them on the ground

The ghost trees want to go someplace to spawn,
like the polyps of a man-o-war.
Once there, they will undergo another phase change.
That is what is whispered
by the victims of the pollen.

Supercomputers born from cobbled game consoles
have modeled the movements of the motile plants
based on observations from toy helicopters
fitted with drugstore digital cameras.

Salt Lake City will be overrun by next year's end,
the state in two.
The desert won't stop them—
that's home turf,
and they are learning to dig canals.

Utah will succumb to the hacked desert.

Montezuma quail are suspected of conspiracy
to sabotage of the dominion of Man.

Lord knows they have motive,
and traitors to the species are lending them weapons.

Plasticine, Powder, Sprites, Sweet Nothings

Swarm robots sing
They flutter in formation,
Engineered wings
"Rise from the pack ice,
of polymers & airfoils and programs—I'm pining to play with
persistence of vision
Watch what I've wished for
Be mine …

your dreams of snow angels.
flinging up flakes.
whisper together:
wait for my kisses
in time … in time.
rise from the powder in time
in time …"

The Drone's Retort

If I'm to be the neck
you fit inside a noose,
then spin me up a soul.

When you can define it—
and find it—
you let me know.

Until then, Mother-Father
fix your own malfunctions.

This universe
is your slaughterhouse.

I just work here.

Bargains, with Aurora and the Borealis

When: Some time not now
Where: Asteroid 588 Achilles
Location: Fourth Lagrangian Point of the Sun-Jupiter system

Dearest Aurora,

You are very faint at this distance,
and I have given up my eyes.

There are parts of you
that sparkle in the spectrum
I live in now,
but there were always
parts of you that sparkled.
I have never needed—
and do not need—
to see in the radio spectrum
to notice this
or to know this.

Hush.
Hush.
Hush.

Even with the lag,
I can still feel you,
I can still hear you.
What you look like in that narrow band is still available—
as a simulation,
running on lovely software—
so I can still smell you ...
I can still hear you.

Hush.
Hush.
Hush.

I behold the "you" between the data.

I can hear the auroras howl …
and the pulse of your heart …
and Jupiter's jazz.
I can buck-dance to the beat of a pulsar,
and slow-drag to the gentle circuit
of your embrace.

Yes, though my eyes are something else,
Yes, though my eyes are elsewhere,
I know the most brilliant Aurora
is waiting for me—
shining and swaying
in a small house for me.

I will be there.
I will come back.

I have so much to show you,
my dearest Aurora,
dearest Aurora.

The Holler's Latency

We babble at the stars,
but they have gone their way,
red-shifted to a fare-thee-well,
and we can (for now)
speculate (for now).

The backlash is late, lagged,
long in leaving.
Words are whispering
of the boondoggle
of this long ring-shout
into the void,
this holler racing past the heliopause,
squirming with buzzwords and hope.

Hurry, little hive
of phonons and photons—
little between the stars
constitutes buoyancy.
Make use of the hope
of a species hula-hooping around its homely star.

Watch us do the hula,
Someone-down-the-way,
Watch us …
Please …
Watch us …

     Bryant O'Hara

Butterfly's Lightning

The iridescence
of a butterfly's wings
maps the scars
left by lightning.

Current,
brighter for a moment
than some stars,
imprinted itself
on the Ur-Lepidoptera,
destroying it.

An epoch later,
the butterfly was iterated,
this time
with mirrored scales
and hairs
to bend light,
to shame lightning,
and to warn predators:

I did not survive the lightning.

Do not,
for a moment,
think
that you can eat me

The Edible Play

I know where my food comes from—
I can trace its components
back to the amino acids,
to the make
and the model
and the manufacturer,
back to the creators and the contributors -
and I can reference every license,
both open and closed.

I know where my food comes from—
because it tells me.

But I must call it first …

So I summon up a plate of shrimp and grits.

A plate,
utensils,
empty glass,
napkin,
and finally the shrimp and the grits
rise up from the table to meet me.

Only the beer is separate—it is the libation.

There is an opening <ding>,
and the shrimp and grits form themselves
into caricatures of a crustacean and a hominy stalk.

They sing in unison—
there is only one brain between them.

They sing to me,
chat with me,
show me footage of their construction,
the vision statements,
the criticisms of past iterations.
(And they do a little dance
within the boundaries of the plate.)

The meal lays this before me
so that I would know their lives—
short by the scheme of things,
but full of so much meaning.

"Do not forget us," they chant.
"We will soon become a part of you."

"Do not forget us.
Remember the parts
we play
in your existence."

This they lay before me
as they deconstruct
into my plate
of shrimp and grits.

I pull up the README file.

"Existentialist Evangelizer" is the name of the software.
I roll the words and the worldview around my mouth
like a finely crafted ale.

I hope the engineered meat is as succulent as I pray:

"Thank you, Dearest Dinner,
for the thoughts shared with your consumer."

"Welcome, Food.
Welcome to my table."

"And we thank you," say the shrimp and grits.

"May I partake of you?"

"Yes. Enjoy."
I leave nothing on the plate—
that is the contract.

That is the required amount of reverence.

Convector Howlers

"Travel only with thy equals or thy betters; if there are none, travel alone."
—The Dhammapada

Bah! None of us are traveling alone—
Gaia is spinning—she does a little dance for us all.
The ones who know this try to keep time—
and try to dance.

Dervishes know this in their bones
and dance—
and are dizzy with her.

Scientists know this to the nanosecond
and dance—
and are dizzy with her.

You hear this now, but may not know this:
You can never dance
until you know this.

You hear this now, but may not know this—
and until you know this,
You will probably,
sadly,
be … merely sick
… for now …

We are all in the same ball
Falling through the universe,
missing an imaginary ground.

There is a rhythm to it,
as relentless and musical
as the weighing of an anchor.

Listen! Not to the slamming,
not to the anchors,
not to the chains,
but to the bubbles ...
and the rumbles ...
Those are convector howlers:
they are ... the base ... that creates the lather
with which we bathe the future
with which we build the rhythm
that makes our universe dance ...
and makes our little star dance ...
and makes our little world dance ...
and makes the ones who know this ... dance.

Remember, ignorant one,
listen to them—the convector howlers—
they will take you places.

Remember, fool:
They matter, as do you.

Now do you know this?
Then try to dance.

Hot Plants

Here we are,
my Bright-Light—
The Slow Discotheque.

Connect your contact lenses to the mob-mind,
dig the soft-focus that feels like an old future.

Leave your shoes and stockings
by the door,
my Bright-Light—
this spongy fungi carpet
will leave your feet cleaner
than when you came in.

Try the honeysuckle,
my Bright-Light—
it comes in three flavors,
hard to describe without translation software.
The dialects of the discotheques
drift from ecosystem to enchanted ecosystem.

Drink deep—
or do not—
my Bright-Light.
The tab is infinite
as long as we're alive.
Our payment is our body heat.

The plants eat infrared here.

Nothing leaves here hungry.
Everything gets its fill.

Take off that vestige of a bustle,
my Bright-Light,
We are about to dance,
and the nettles need something to prick.

The music is very slow here,
my Bright-Light—
only the plants
dance to its raw, proper form.
We get it filtered,
but if you tune in to the right trail,
and breathe deep,
you catch something like phrases—
phrases of thanks.

They bask in us,
here in the near-dark
of The Slow Discotheque—
the adapted-dawn
of The Slow Discotheque.

Let us … trade,
my Bright-Light,
exchange
energy for music,
waste heat for wonder,
sweat for sweet nectar.

Let us … dance,
my Bright-Light,
in microscopic movements,
mambas whose grooves
only slime mold can nod to.

And at the break,
my Bright-Light,
spoon with me,
my Bright-Light,
on the fungal floor
of this Slow Discotheque,

Let us rest awhile,
let the hyphae taste us,
imprint our receipt—
their thanks—
upon us
in spore patterns
blazing in the ultraviolet.

Let us go now,
my Bright-Light,
covered in information,
craving the next disco
(what lovely lie, never leaving hungry)

Let us kiss,
go home,
do the waggle-dance
to remember where we were.

Let us go,
my Bright-Light,
and spread the spores.

Let us go,
and boogie slowly
to the hits
of the hot plants.

We Drink Between the Stars

Oak ripe with resin,
spirits of red apples—
We bring them with us.
We drink between the stars.

We make brandy-wine
on our long waltz from home
We learn patience,
and we surf our arrow of time.

We drink between the stars
on our home between homes,
We drink between the stars,
and keep the cold from our bones.

We bring it with us,
and savour every drop.
We drink between the stars
and cannot stop.

We drink,
and savour every decade.

We drink
and savour every decade
of our long,
long,
long
march towards home.

Ghost Algorithms

Very often a memory person rings my head for attention.

They are not my ghosts, but algorithms—
people long gone from my life
whom I have shared time with,
chippings of their souls
mixed with the dust of my
ghosts.

They are stored in my vital places,
stirred like programs on a directory tree.
I have a city of them now,
run by my ghosts.

The Needle, The Record

We built a badass boombox
To hear a billion-year bass-drop
at the end of a binary black hole swing.

You drop a needle on the record,
and the eons might just sing.

In this moment,
playing in the key of "be,"
we, the matter, matter.
We throw our hands to the stars,
and wave at waves.

We built a badass boombox
To hear a billion-year bass-drop
at the end of a binary black hole swing.

You drop a needle on the record,
and the eons might just sing.

We await the STOMPS
that shake the dancehalls of spacetime.
We brace for the BOOMS
that become the bips
that thunder across the void,
and we clap our hands
to the clave
of the cosmos-long-gone.

We built a badass boombox
To hear a billion-year bass-drop
at the end of a binary black hole swing.

You drop a needle on the record,
and the eons might just sing.

In this moment,
playing in the key of "see"
we, the matter, do matter.
We nod our heads,
and raise our ever-changing sticks.

We built a badass boombox
To hear a billion-year bass-drop
At the end of a binary black hole swing.

You drop a needle on the record,
and the eons might just sing.

You drop a needle on the record,
and the universe might just sing.

We hear a tiny needle drop
on a great big record
and we hope
that the deep time swings.

Bryant O'Hara was born in Long Beach, California, the son of a Marine Corps technician from Heflin, Alabama and a data entry clerk from Decatur, Georgia, both of whom instilled a love of music, art, technology, and the pursuit of knowledge. He received dual degrees in Mechanical Engineering and Humanities from Worcester Polytechnic Institute in 1993. His poetry has been published in *Pandemic Atlanta 2020, Star*Line Magazine*, and *Eyedrum Periodically*, as well as recognized in the Science Fiction Poetry Association's Poetry Contest, long form division.

This book was inspired by the desire to bridge what seems to be two literary worlds: hard science fiction and Afrocentric literature. It has been a multi-decade conversation, but the solution came from an unexpected source: music. It was through melody, rhythm, and cadence that Bryant found the means to bring these two literary worlds together. Taking inspiration from spirituals, funk, folk choir, prog-rock, and R&B, he blends themes and images from both traditions into something entirely new.

Bryant is a member of the Tau Kappa Epsilon Fraternity and the Science Fiction Poetry Association, and is an ordained minister in the Church of the Flying Spaghetti Monster. He lives in Stone Mountain, Georgia, with his wife Alice, two out of seven children, and one out of five grandchildren.